Practice Makes Perfect

Text and jacket art by

Rosemary Wells

Interior illustrations by

Jody Wheeler

VOLO

Hyperion Books for Children

New York

Printed in the United States of America

First Edition
1 3 5 7 9 10 8 6 4 2

LIBRARY OF CONGRESS CATALOGING-IN-PUBLICATION DATA
Wells, Rosemary.
Practice makes perfect / text and jacket art by Rosemary Wells; interior illustrations by Jody Wheeler.—1st ed.
p.   cm. — (Yoko and friends—school days)
Summary: Yoko helps Timothy learn to play the bells of Sarna so that he can
perform a solo in the school talent show.
ISBN 0-7868-0725-3 (hc.) — ISBN 0-7868-1531-0 (pbk.)
[1. Music—Fiction. 2. Schools—Fiction. 3. Bells—Fiction. 4. Badgers—Fiction.
5. Cats—Fiction. 6. Japanese Americans—Fiction.] I. Wheeler, Jody, ill. II. Title.
PZ7.W46843 Pr 2002
[E]—dc21
2001057510

Visit www.hyperionchildrensbooks.com

"I want to play a solo in the class
talent show!" said Timothy.

In the music corner, Timothy
played the coffee cans.

Bang! Whang! Spang!

"I can play the loudest music

of all!" said Timothy.

Yoko played a note on her violin.

"I can't hear you!" said Timothy.

"I can't hear me, either!" said Yoko.

"I can't hear *anything* when you're
smacking and whacking on the
coffee cans like that."

"Timothy," said Mrs. Jenkins,

"if you play so loud,

we won't hear Yoko's music!"

"I want to play by myself

in the talent show, like Yoko!"

said Timothy.

"We have two solo players,

Timothy," said Mrs. Jenkins.

"They are Yoko and Claude.

Yoko and Claude can read music.

Can you read music, Timothy?"

"I can read anything!" said Timothy.

"Oh," said Timothy. "I mean,

I can *play* anything."

"Can you play 'Twinkle,

Twinkle'?" asked Mrs. Jenkins.

"Oh, sure," said Timothy.

"That is easy."

"Very good," said Mrs. Jenkins.

"Let's hear you both play

'Twinkle, Twinkle.'"

Yoko played the song very softly

and very sweetly.

Timothy hit the coffee cans

as hard as he could.

"Timothy," said Mrs. Jenkins,

"when we play music, everybody

must be heard. Maybe you should

try the triangle instead."

"Charles plays triangle,"

said Timothy.

"How about the tin whistle?"

asked Mrs. Jenkins.

"Lily plays the tin whistle,"

said Timothy.

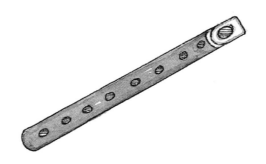

"How about the bells of Sarna?"

asked Mrs. Jenkins.

"I will play the bells,"

said Timothy.

All the way home on the school

bus, Timothy rang the bells.

He jingled them all at once.

"Stop that dinging and ringing!"

yelled the Franks.

"I am making beautiful music!"
said Timothy.

"It is a beautiful noise," said Yoko,

"but it is not music.

Why don't we try it out at

my house?"

At Yoko's house, Yoko and

Timothy sat on a tatami mat.

Yoko's mother served red-bean

ice cream and sweet tea to

Yoko and Timothy.

Timothy rang the bells.

"Pretty bells!" said Yoko's mother.

"Try one at a time."

Timothy found that each

of the bells sounded different.

"You have eight bells," said Yoko.

"One bell for each note.

For 'Twinkle, Twinkle'

we'll use six of the bells."

"Can you read music,

Timothy?" asked Yoko.

"What do you mean?"

asked Timothy.

"I can teach you if you want,"

said Yoko.

"Sure," said Timothy.

She arranged three bells like this:

"Start with bell at the left.

"Ring each bell twice.

Then ring the middle one once."

Timothy rang the bells just as

Yoko had placed them.

"It's 'Twinkle, Twinkle, Little Star'!"

said Timothy.

"Soon you will be able to read

music, too!" said Yoko.

Yoko showed Timothy her music

book.

"See!" she said. "The notes go up,

the notes go down.

They are not so different

from the bells on the mat."

Timothy was so excited, he played

"Twinkle, Twinkle" all afternoon.

"I want to play the next part,"

said Timothy.

"Tomorrow," said Yoko,

"we will do it!"

That night Timothy practiced his

bells in bed.

Timothy rang his bells until

his mother and father peeked

in the door.

"Timothy!" they said. "We cannot

sleep! Enough bells until morning!"

The next day, Timothy played his bells for Mrs. Jenkins.

"Today I will learn the second part of the song," said Timothy.

After school, Yoko's mother served
yellow-bean cakes. This time, Yoko
put four bells out on the mat.

"Ring each one twice," said Yoko,
"except the last bell. The last bell
is one long ring."

"That's easy!" said Timothy.

Timothy played the song until he
got it right five times in a row.

"Tell me the rest of it, Yoko!" he
said. "I want to play a solo in the
talent show!"

A week later, Yoko told

Mrs. Jenkins, "Timothy is ready to

play a solo on the bells of Sarna!"

"Wonderful, Timothy!" said Mrs.

Jenkins. "I can't wait to hear it!"

Timothy put three bells out.

He played, "1 1 5 5 6 6 5."

Then he stopped. He set four bells

out the second way.

He played, "4 4 3 3 2 2 1."

Timothy played the whole song,

stopping sometimes to move

the bells.

"Can you play it all together?" asked Mrs. Jenkins.

"No," said Timothy, "because I must use one of the bells over again in different places."

"If you can remember how to play the whole song without stopping," said Mrs. Jenkins, "you can play a solo in the class talent show."

That afternoon, Yoko put

Timothy's bells out in a row.

Then she put a piece of tape on

each bell.

She marked the bells

1, 2, 3, 4, 5, and 6.

Then she made lines across a piece

of paper and filled in the numbers.

Just like this:

1	1	5	5		6	6	5
4	4	3	3		2	2	1
5	5	4	4	3		3	2
5	5	4	4	3		3	2
1	1	5	5		6	6	5
4	4	3	3		2	2	1

"See!" said Yoko. "Each bell has a

number. Look at the paper and

ring the bell for that number."

Timothy did.

"That was easy!" said Timothy.

He played the whole song again

and again.

Timothy played his solo in the

class talent show. He played it

perfectly.

His parents were so proud.

"You are a wonderful musician,
Timothy," said Mrs. Jenkins.
"And you, Yoko, are a wonderful
music teacher."

Dear Parents,

When our children were young we lived in a small house, but we always made a space just for books. When their dad or I would read a story out loud, the TV was always off—radio and music, too—because it intruded.

Soon this peaceful half hour of every day became like a little island vacation. Our children are lifetime readers now, with an endless curiosity for the rich world waiting between the covers of good books. It cost us nothing but time well spent and a library card.

This set of easy-to-read books is about the real nitty-gritty of elementary school. There are new friends, and bullies, too. There are germs and the "Clean Hands" song, new ways of painting pictures, learning music, telling the truth, gossiping, teasing, laughing, crying, separating from Mama, scary Halloweens, and secret valentines. The stories are all drawn from the experiences my children had in school.

It's my hope that these books will transport you and your children to a setting that's familiar, yet new, a place where you can explore the exciting new world of school together.

Rosemary Wells